Kate DiCamillo
Mercy Watson
Princess in Disguise

illustrated by Chris Van Dusen

CANDLEWICK PRESS

First paperback edition 2010

The Library of Congress has cataloged the hardcover edition as follows:

DiCamillo, Kate.
Mercy Watson: princess in disguise / Kate DiCamillo ;
illustrated by Chris Van Dusen. —1st ed.
p.   cm.
Summary: Persuaded by the word "treating" to
dress up as a princess for Halloween, Mercy the pig's
trick-or-treat outing has some very unexpected results.
ISBN 978-0-7636-3014-0 (hardcover)
[1. Pigs—Fiction. 2. Halloween—Fiction. 3. Humorous stories.]
I. Van Dusen, Chris, ill. II. Title.
PZ7.D5455Mpd 2007
[Fic]—dc22   2006051827

ISBN 978-0-7636-4951-7 (paperback)

10 11 12 13 14 15 CCP 10 9 8 7 6 5 4 3 2 1

Printed in Shenzhen, Guangdong, China

This book was typeset in Mrs. Eaves.
The illustrations were done in gouache.

Candlewick Press
99 Dover Street
Somerville, Massachusetts 02144

visit us at www.candlewick.com

For Max, who would follow Mercy anywhere
K. D.

In memory of my Gram,
maker of the most extraordinary costumes
C. V.

Chapter

1

Mr. Watson and Mrs. Watson have a pig named Mercy.

Mr. Watson, Mrs. Watson, and Mercy live together in a house at 54 Deckawoo Drive.

One October afternoon, in the living room of the house on Deckawoo Drive, Mrs. Watson had an idea.

"Darling," said Mrs. Watson.

"Yes?" said Mr. Watson.

"Halloween is coming."

"It most certainly is," said Mr. Watson.

"I believe that Mercy should dress up," said Mrs. Watson.

Mercy opened one eye.

"I believe that Mercy should dress up and go trick-or-treating," said Mrs. Watson.

Mercy opened both eyes.

She liked, very much, the sound of the word "treating."

"What a splendid idea!" said Mr. Watson. "But what should Mercy be?"

Chapter
2

Should Mercy be a ghost?” asked
Mr. Watson.

"I don't think so," said Mrs. Watson.

"A pumpkin?"

"Not quite right," said Mrs. Watson.

"A pirate?

"A robot?

"A witch?"

"No, no, no," said Mrs. Watson.

Mercy sighed.

She closed her eyes.

She fell asleep.

"What, then?" asked Mr. Watson. "What should Mercy be?"

"I am quite certain," said Mrs. Watson, "that Mercy should be a princess."

"Of course!" said Mr. Watson. "It is obvious. Why didn't I think of that?"

"You must go and find her a tiara,"

said Mrs. Watson. "And I will make her
a princess dress."

"I am on the case," said Mr. Watson.

"Oh, Mercy," said Mrs. Watson,
"you will be so lovely. You will be
beautiful beyond compare."

Chapter 3

Mrs. Watson measured Mercy from snout to tail.

She measured her from side to side.

She measured Mercy around and around and around.

"Heavens," said Mrs. Watson. "I hope I have enough fabric."

When Mercy woke up from her nap, Mrs. Watson was smiling at her.

"Darling," said Mrs. Watson, "your dress is finished."

"Oink," said Mercy.

"I know," said Mrs. Watson. "It is stunning, isn't it? Let's try it on."

Mrs. Watson put Mercy's right front leg into the dress.

Mercy took her right front leg out.

Mrs. Watson put Mercy's left front leg into the dress.

Mercy took her left front leg out.

"Goodness gracious!" said Mrs. Watson. "Please hold still or we will never get this dress on."

"My darlings, my dears," called Mr. Watson, "I am home! And I have located the tiara!"

"Oh, Mr. Watson," said Mrs. Watson. "I am having a difficult time here. Mercy does not want to wear her princess dress."

"Perhaps," said Mr. Watson, "you should tell her about the treats."

Chapter
4

Mercy pricked up her ears.

She liked treats.

Her favorite treat of all was toast with a great deal of butter on it.

"My darling, my dear," said Mr. Watson, "if you wear this dress, everyone in the neighborhood will give you treats."

Mercy closed her eyes.

She could see it quite clearly.

"But if you want the treats, you must wear the dress," said Mr. Watson.

Mercy sighed.

She allowed Mrs. Watson to put her left front leg and her right front leg into the dress.

She allowed Mrs. Watson to zip the dress up.

She allowed Mr. Watson to put the tiara on her head.

"Utterly regal," said Mrs. Watson.

"A porcine vision," said Mr. Watson.

Mercy's stomach growled.

She was looking forward to the treats.

Chapter
5

On Halloween night, the doorbell rang at the Lincoln Sisters' house.

"Sister," called Baby Lincoln, "somebody is at the door."

"Of course somebody is at the door," said Eugenia. "It is Halloween. People are expected to be at the door when it is Halloween."

"Mowl," said General Washington, Eugenia Lincoln's new cat.

"Trick or treat!" shouted Mr. Watson and Mrs. Watson.

"Oink!" said Mercy.

"Mercy is a princess," said Mr. Watson.

"She looks exactly like a princess," said Baby.

"She looks like a pig in a cheap dress," said Eugenia.

"Oh, Sister," said Baby.

"In my opinion," said Eugenia, "pigs should not go trick-or-treating. In my opinion, pigs should not pose as princesses."

"Mowl," said General Washington.

"Oh, dear," said Baby Lincoln.

Eugenia Lincoln slammed the door.

Chapter
6

Eugenia seems upset," said Mr. Watson.

"Yes," said Mrs. Watson. "She does."

Mercy's stomach growled.

Where are the treats? she wondered.

Where is the toast?

"Look," said Mr. Watson. "I think that Baby is trying to tell us something."

"Oink," said Mercy.

She kicked up her heels.

She ran around to the back of the

Lincoln Sisters' house.

"Follow that princess!" said Mr.

Watson.

25

Chapter
7

Baby Lincoln was waiting at the back door.

"Shhhhh," she said. "I'm afraid that Sister is not in a Halloween sort of mood. But I could not let you leave without your treats."

"Yum," said Mr. Watson.

"What a delightful array," said Mrs. Watson. "What shall we choose, Mercy?"

Diiiiiing Doooong

"Baby!" shouted Eugenia. "Where is that treat bowl?"

"I'm on my way, Sister," shouted Baby.

"Hurry! Hurry!" Baby said. "Take something!"

Mercy examined the treats closely.

She did not see one single piece of toast.

But she did detect the faintest hint of
butter.

Butter, thought Mercy.

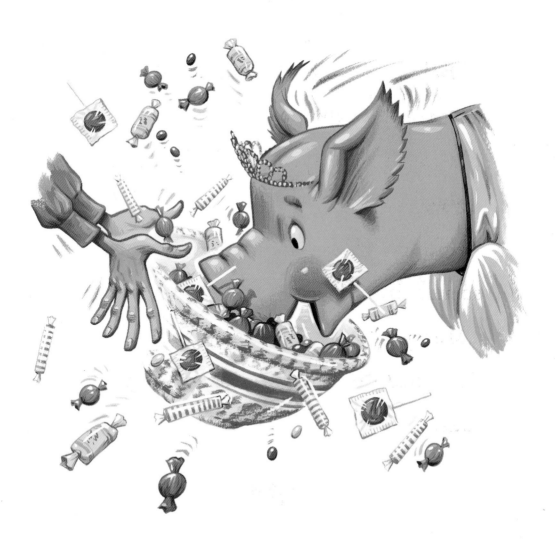

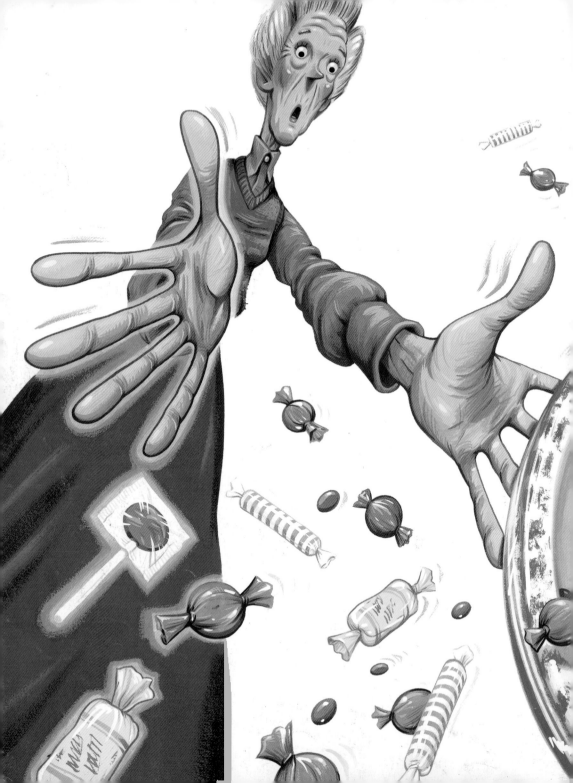

"Oh," said Baby. "Mercy!"

Chapter 8

Oink," said Mercy.

She snuffled the floor.

There was a lot of candy.

There was a lot of candy everywhere.

Candy was not toast, but it would

have to do.

Mercy munched a lollipop.

She ate a lemon drop.

She chewed a caramel.

"What is going on here?" shouted Eugenia. "Why is the candy on the floor? And what is that *pig* doing in my kitchen?"

"She's not a pig," said Mr. Watson. "She's a princess."

Mercy crunched a Butter Barrel.

Mmm, thought Mercy. *Butter.*

Chapter
9

Get out of my kitchen immediately!"
screamed Eugenia Lincoln.

"Well," said Mr. Watson, "I think it
might be time for us to skedaddle."

"Yes, indeed," said Mrs. Watson.
"We still have quite a lot of trick-or-
treating to do. Come along, Mercy."

Mercy was eating her second Butter
Barrel.

It was delicious.

And there were many more Butter
Barrels on the floor.

"Mooowwl," said General
Washington.

He swatted at the ruffle on Mercy's
dress.

"Yip!" said Mercy.

General Washington took a swipe at
Mercy's tiara.

"Yow!" said Mercy.

"The cat!" said Mr. Watson.

"The pig!" said Eugenia Lincoln.

"Oh, dear," said Baby Lincoln.

The cat ran out of the kitchen.

The pig ran after him.

It was a chase.

Mercy loved a chase.

Chapter
10

General Washington ran.

Mercy ran after General Washington.

Eugenia ran after Mercy.

Baby ran after Eugenia.

Mr. Watson ran after Baby.

Mrs. Watson ran after Mr. Watson.

"Moowwwwwwwwll," said General Washington.

"Oink!" said Mercy.

"Pig!" said Eugenia.

"Sister!" said Baby.

"Darling!" said Mr. Watson.

"Dear!" said Mrs. Watson.

41

General Washington ran through
the living room and back into the
kitchen.

He ran out the open back door.

Mercy was in hot pursuit.

Her dress felt a bit snug. But it did not slow her down.

She was having an excellent time.

Chapter
11

Frank and Stella are brother and sister. Frank and Stella live at 50 Deckawoo Drive.

"Look at that," said Stella.

"What is it?" asked Frank.

"It's a Halloween parade," said Stella.

"Stand back," said Frank. "It looks dangerous."

"Wait for me!" Stella shouted. "I want to be in the parade, too."

"Stella!" shouted Frank.

"Stelllllllllllllllaaaaaaaaaaaaaaaa!"

Chapter
12

General Washington raced to the end
of Deckawoo Drive.

He ran up the trunk of an old
oak tree.

Mercy stopped.

Behind Mercy, Eugenia did not stop.

Eugenia bumped into Mercy.

Baby bumped into Eugenia.

Mr. Watson bumped into Baby.

Mrs. Watson bumped into Mr. Watson.

Stella bumped into Mrs. Watson.

And Frank bumped into Stella.

Mercy looked up at General
Washington.

She sighed.

She sat down.

The chase was over.

Mercy was very tired.

She was very hot.

Her tiara was pinching her ears.

Her pink dress felt terribly snug.

And even porcine princesses cannot climb trees.

Chapter
13

Well," said Stella, "I guess the parade is over."

"Nothing is over!" Eugenia Lincoln shouted.

She stared up into the branches of the tree.

"General Washington," said Eugenia, "come down here immediately."

"Moowwll," said General
Washington.

"General Washington," said
Eugenia, "I will not take 'no' for an
answer."

"Moowwwwllllllll," said General
Washington.

"Cats don't usually do what you ask
them to do," said Stella.

"Nonsense," said Eugenia.
"General Washington always obeys
orders."

"I think that cat is stuck," said Frank.

"Nonsense," said Eugenia. "General Washington is far too intelligent to get stuck."

Eugenia called General Washington again.

And again.

But General Washington would not move.

"I think," said Mr. Watson, "it might be a good time to call the fire department."

Chapter
14

At the fire station, the phone rang.
Ned took the call.

"How's that?" said Ned.

"General Washington?" said Ned.

"Stuck up a tree?" said Ned.

"Right," said Ned. "We're on our
way."

"That was a strange call," Ned said
to Lorenzo. "Apparently a general is
stuck in a tree."

"Hmmmm," said Lorenzo. "What is
the address?"

"Somewhere on Deckawoo Drive," said Ned.

"Deckawoo Drive?" said Lorenzo. "That is where the pig lives."

"Oh, boy," said Ned. "We'd better hurry."

Chapter
15

When Ned and Lorenzo got to Deckawoo Drive, they saw a large oak tree.

Underneath the oak tree was a pig in a pink dress with a tiara on her head.

"It is just as I suspected," said Lorenzo. "There is that pig."

"Yes," said Ned, "but where is General Washington?"

"Thank goodness you are here," said Baby Lincoln.

"What took you so long?" said Eugenia Lincoln.

"Is that General Washington?" said Ned.

He pointed to the gray cat high in the oak tree.

"Of course it is," said Eugenia Lincoln.

"Mooooooowwwwwwwwwwlllllllll," said General Washington.

Lorenzo got a ladder from the truck.

He leaned the ladder against the tree.

He climbed up the ladder.

He reached out and grabbed hold of
General Washington.

He climbed down the ladder.

He put General Washington into Eugenia's arms.

"Hooray!" everyone cheered.

"You can always count on the fire department," said Mr. Watson. "That is what I say."

"Oh," said Mrs. Watson, "we should celebrate. We should have a party."

Mercy pricked up her ears.

Parties, in Mercy's experience, almost always involved toast.

Chapter
16

Everyone was in the Watsons' kitchen.

Everyone was gathered around the Watsons' table.

"Have you ever had the toast here?" Lorenzo asked Stella.

"No," said Stella.

"You are in for a treat," said Ned. "The toast here is excellent."

"Eating food at a stranger's house is potentially dangerous," said Frank.

"But we are not strangers," said Mrs. Watson. "We are your neighbors."

"Moooowwwwwwwwwwwwwwwllll," said General Washington.

"Bah," said Eugenia Lincoln, "who needs neighbors?"

"Oh, Sister," said Baby. "Here, have a Butter Barrel."

"My darling, my dear, my porcine princess," said Mr. Watson, "aren't you glad you put on the pink dress?"

Mercy put her snout up in the air. She sniffed.

Bread was toasting! Butter was melting!

The pink dress was terribly snug.

But it was worth it.

"Oink!" said Mercy.

"Happy Halloween, my darling!" said Mr. Watson. "Happy Halloween, everyone!"

Kate DiCamillo is the renowned author of numerous books for young readers, including all of the Mercy Watson stories. About *Mercy Watson: Princess in Disguise,* she says, "Mercy and Halloween seem like a match made in heaven: treats, treats everywhere! And all you have to do to get them is dress up like a princess! As an aside, Mercy would like to express her profound belief that hot buttered toast would make an excellent trick-or-treat item." Kate DiCamillo lives in Minneapolis.

Chris Van Dusen is the author-illustrator of *Down to the Sea with Mr. Magee, A Camping Spree with Mr. Magee, If I Built a Car,* and *The Circus Ship.* About *Mercy Watson: Princess in Disguise,* he says, "It's been an absolute joy to work on these pictures for this series, but Mercy in her Halloween costume takes the cake. I must have the best job in the world—painting pictures of pigs in pink tutus!" Chris Van Dusen lives in Maine.

Join Mercy Watson

in all six of her pig tales!

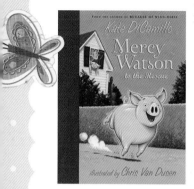

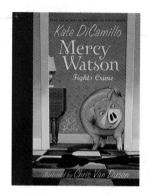

 1   Mercy Watson
to the Rescue

 2   Mercy Watson
Goes for a Ride

 3   Mercy Watson
Fights Crime

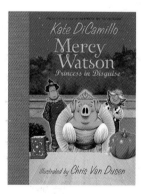

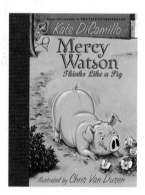

 4   Mercy Watson:
Princess in
Disguise

5   Mercy Watson
Thinks Like a Pig

6   Mercy Watson:
Something Wonky
This Way Comes